Glow in the Dark
Under the Sea

Written by Jean Lewis
Illustrated by Eugenie

A GOLDEN BOOK • NEW YORK
Western Publishing Company, Inc., Racine, Wisconsin 53404

MCMXCII

Judy and Ben left the seaplane and looked around for Aunt Vi. They were going to spend the whole day with Aunt Vi and Uncle Ted in their underwater lab, Shell House.

Aunt Vi was waiting for them in a mini-submarine. They all got in and descended to the ocean floor.

"Welcome aboard," called Uncle Ted when they arrived at Shell House. Uncle Ted was fixing lunch in the galley.

"Welcome aboard," echoed Pierre, a big green parrot.

After a tasty meal of hamburgers and seaweed salad, Judy and Ben fed cookie crumbs to Peter, the pet pilotfish. Judy laughed. "He likes people food!" she said.

"Pilotfish do," said Aunt Vi. "Sometimes they follow ships just for food scraps."

Uncle Ted took Judy and Ben underwater sight-seeing in the mini-sub.

They visited a coral reef. A hungry parrotfish was chewing off chunks of coral, while inside the reef nighttime fish slept. A small clown fish had the softest bed, snoozing in the velvety petals of a sea anemone. Three young angelfish were eating tiny parasites off the back of a surgeonfish.

Farther down, Ben and Judy met some odd bottom dwellers.
A searobin "walked" by, using its large fins as feet.
As the children watched, a fluke quickly changed color to match
its background. This camouflage completely fooled the barn-door
skate chasing it. The larger fish swam right over the fluke!

Suddenly a torpedo ray bumped into the side of the sub. Uncle Ted told them the two electric cells in its head were powerful enough to stun a person.

Soon they came to the wreck of a sailing ship. Uncle Ted had explored it in his scuba gear.

"We hoped it was Captain Kidd's pirate ship," he said.

"Did you find any treasure?" asked Ben.

"No treasure," said Uncle Ted, "just empty molasses kegs." Then suddenly he pointed. "Look, a stowaway!"

An octopus uncoiled itself from a keg to look for a crab dinner.

As Judy peered into the shadows of the wreck, she saw
mysterious flickering lights. "It looks as though there are
ghosts in there," she said.

Uncle Ted showed Judy that her ghostly lights came from
tiny lanternfish, whose sides glow in the dark as they swim.

Suddenly—*thwack!*—something hit the rear Plexiglas window with a powerful blow. The submarine lurched violently.

There, outside the window, waved the mighty tail of a fifteen-foot thresher shark. The shark was annoyed to find the sub between it and a fish dinner!

Uncle Ted quickly steered away from the eight-hundred-pound shark and brought the sub safely back to Shell House.

"I hope the window isn't cracked," said Uncle Ted, looking worried. "I'll have to make sure it's watertight or we can't use the sub."

While Uncle Ted examined the window, Aunt Vi introduced
Judy and Ben to the sea creatures in the Shell House aquarium.

Then Aunt Vi showed Judy and Ben how to get information on all the different underwater creatures from the computer. From his perch above them, Pierre repeated after her, "Sea star! Sea horse! Butterfly fish!"

Aunt Vi made computer printouts for Judy and Ben to take home.

Judy and Ben were almost disappointed to hear the sub was okay and Aunt Vi could take them to the five o'clock seaplane. It would have been fun to stay overnight in Shell House!

Since there wasn't enough room in the sub, Uncle Ted came up in his wet suit and scuba gear.

"I bet this is the first underwater pet carrier you've seen,"
Uncle Ted said with a laugh as he unsnapped the lid of a big
pressure cooker.

"Welcome aboard!" piped a familiar voice and out hopped
Pierre. He was going to the vet to have his claws and beak trimmed.

There was time for a quick swim. Lots of curious angelfish and butterfly fish came to see Judy and Ben.

At the sound of the plane's engines, Judy and Ben swam to the dock for the flight home. What a wonderful visit it had been!

Back at home, Judy and Ben looked at their aquarium. In it were many of the sea creatures they had seen at Shell House. Now they could identify them all.

That night Judy and Ben fell asleep in the soft glow of the aquarium's light, to dream of more wonderful adventures under the sea.